Tales from

Around
the
World

This edition published by Barnes & Noble, Inc., by arrangement with
Chrysalis Children's Books.

Text and illustrations copyright © 2003 Graham Percy

2003 Barnes & Noble Books

ISBN 0-7607-4770-9

Printed and bound in Singapore

10 9 8 7 6 5 4 3 2 1

TALES FROM
AROUND
THE
WORLD

RETOLD AND ILLUSTRATED BY
Graham Percy

BARNES
&NOBLE
BOOKS
NEW YORK

For Lucie and Noah

Contents

THE AMAZING TEA-KETTLE

A TALE FROM JAPAN

THERE WAS ONCE an old priest who lived beside a ramshackle temple not far from a little village. Nearby, some of the villagers would leave all sorts of things they no longer wanted or needed. This was the very place, on top of the pile of bits and pieces, that the old man found a tea-kettle. It was dented and dirty but the priest was a careful man and he set to work cleaning and polishing it until it shone like the sun. Then he filled the kettle with water and put it on the fire to boil. Soon it was singing away and the lid was bouncing up and down merrily.

Then the most amazing thing happened. All at once, the kettle started to change into a badger! First, there came the head, then four legs and finally the tail.

6

And, in no time at all, this badger was dancing all around the room. The old man cried out for a younger priest and, together, they managed to catch the badger before it pranced out through the door. They bundled the animal into a box and tied down the lid with some thick rope. The old priest was so exhausted by all the excitement that he lay down and went off to sleep.

In the morning, as soon as he woke up, the priest untied the rope and peeped inside the box. But the badger had gone! Instead, there was the tea-kettle: it had lost its shine and was battered and dirty once more.

"What a stupid thing," grumbled the old priest, carrying the box outside.

But he didn't throw it onto the garbage heap. No, he continued to the village where he sold his kettle to a shopkeeper.

"I can't give you much for this old piece of junk," said the man, tossing a few coins onto the counter. The priest was sure that his kettle was worth more but he took the money without a word, not knowing how to explain his strange story to the shopkeeper.

That night it was the shopkeeper's turn to be amazed. He had not been asleep for long when he was woken by a rustling and a pit-patting. It was coming from the corner where he had left the priest's box and, by the light of the moon, he could just make out a badger dancing and leaping about!

All night the badger danced, on and on. Sometimes it stood on its head, sometimes it whirled around on the tip of its toes and, all the while, its eyes glowed like two orange lanterns. The shopkeeper hid under his padded quilt and waited anxiously for morning.

As soon as it was light, he shuffled nervously over to the corner of his shop – only to find the kettle in its box again.

Rushing into the shop next door, quite out of breath, the man told his neighbor what had happened during the night. His friend looked very thoughtful and, stroking his chin, whispered, "There's money to be made from this old kettle of yours."

The very next day the two shopkeepers put up a tent and painted a sign that said, "Come inside to see the magic tea-kettle perform!" And indeed all the villagers *did* come – men, women and children. First, they paid at a little kiosk outside. Then, taking off their shoes, they entered the tent and sat down on straw mats to watch the performance.

And what a performance it was! First the kettle would sing, with its lid bobbing up and down and then, of course, it would start to change into the badger. Children and adults alike clapped with delight as the badger danced upon the stage – sometimes standing on its head and sometimes on its tail. It even waltzed daintily across a tightrope! Then, at the end of each day's final performance, the badger would shrivel up into a dirty tea-kettle once more.

In no time the two shopkeepers became very rich, but neither of them had quite forgotten the old priest.

"I didn't really pay him much for such an amazing tea-kettle," said the first shopkeeper to the other.

"Let's go out to his temple and give him his proper reward," replied his friend. And not only did they give the old priest a trunk filled with money, they also returned the dirty old tea-kettle in its box.

The grateful priest cleared away the garbage pile and bought everything he needed to make a beautiful garden. What's more, he had enough money left over to repair his temple and make it much grander than it had ever been before. Somewhere inside, he hid the kettle in a very secret place and it was never seen again. But someday, if you should visit Japan and come across that temple with its beautiful garden, you might even find the amazing tea-kettle, too!

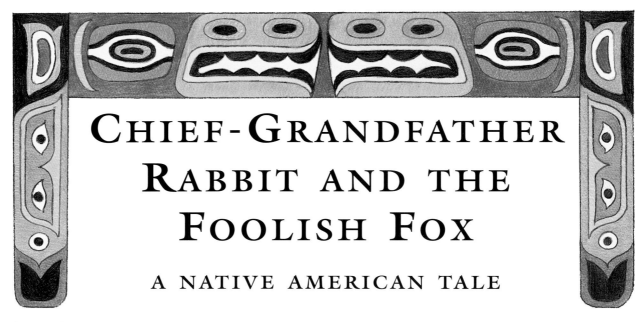

Chief-Grandfather Rabbit and the Foolish Fox

A Native American Tale

THIS STORY TELLS of a time long, long ago, when the world was still new and none of the animals knew one another very well. At that time, set among green hills, there was a little blue lake edged with a narrow strip of yellow sand. All around the lake lived thousands of rabbits. They made their burrows in the sandy soil, they nibbled the short, fine grass and they played all kinds of games on the hillside, with their white tails bobbing everywhere.

And so it was – until the Fox came. He was a young fox from very far away and early one morning he looked down from a high hill and saw the rabbits scampering by the lake, their little white tails bobbing everywhere.

"This seems a very good place for me!" he thought. But as he trotted down the hillside to catch his first plump rabbit – suddenly, they had all disappeared into their burrows. The Fox snarled to himself and sat down to wait for them to come out again. He waited and waited until he was feeling very hungry.

At last, the rabbits that were farthest from the Fox came right out of their burrows and sat washing their faces. Even their little ones came out and scampered around – they all seemed to be showing how little they were worried by the Fox. He, meanwhile, rushed this way and that trying to catch one of them. A large rabbit or a small rabbit or a middle-sized rabbit – any kind of rabbit would do. But he couldn't catch a single one! At last he lay down under a bush for a rest and went off to sleep.

Meanwhile, the rabbits gathered for a meeting.

"We can neither graze nor play safely on the hillside," they agreed, "because this awful creature is waiting to eat us!" So they made a plan.

It was evening when the Fox woke up and began to move. At once the rabbits disappeared into their burrows and the Fox crept down the deserted hillside. Then, from a burrow near the Fox's feet, there came a voice that quite made him jump.

"Good evening," it said politely, "so, you have come back to our lake."

"Yes," snapped the Fox, "I'm back and I'm hungry. And who might you be?"

"I," said the voice, "am the Chief-Grandfather-of-the-Rabbits."

The Fox peered into the burrow where the voice had come from and he could just see a stout rabbit looking at him with large, round eyes.

"And now," continued the Chief-Grandfather Rabbit, ever so politely, "my people and I have a bargain to make with you." His large eyes glowed in the moonlight. "We are tired of eating grass and we've decided we'd like to eat a fox for a change. But we want to be fair – after all, there are many of us and only one of you. So let there be a race between you and me. If you win, you may eat as many of us as you like. But if I win," said the Chief-Grandfather Rabbit gravely, "we shall eat you. Is that a bargain?"

"Yes, yes! Of course!" said the Fox impatiently. He was thinking of his own strong, swift legs. "Where will the race be run?"

"Once around the lake," said the Chief-Grandfather Rabbit. "You shall run on the shore and I shall run underground."

"Hmm... I don't know much about rabbits but I suppose they have roads underground," thought the Fox.

"So, are you ready?" called the Chief-Grandfather Rabbit from deep in his burrow. "Then, let the race begin from here ... GO!"

The Fox started off at a comfortable trot. "Old Grandfather-Big-Eyes won't be able to run for long," he said to himself.

"Come along! Hurry up!" called a voice from a mound in front of him. And there was a stout rabbit with large, round eyes waving at him in the moonlight.

"Dear me," said the Fox. "How did Grandfather-Big-Eyes get that far? I must hurry along." And he began to run faster.

But the voice kept calling. First from the little stream in front of him. Then, farther ahead, from some bushes and, finally, in the distance, from a pile of rocks. Each time it jeered, "Come along! Hurry up!"

17

And each time, he saw those large, round eyes laughing at him before the stout rabbit disappeared back into his burrow to continue the race.

By now the Fox was gasping for breath but he kept going across the moonlit grass as fast as he could. His tongue was hanging out, he was panting hard and his eyes were almost popping out of his head. All around him, the hillsides were covered with rabbits laughing and cheering.

The Fox just couldn't keep up with the Chief-Grandfather Rabbit. He was almost at the finishing line when the Chief-Grandfather Rabbit popped up, brushing himself down and calling back to the Fox, "Dear me, how slowly you run! I have been waiting here forever."

So it was all over. The Chief-Grandfather Rabbit had won, easily. Of course, there were *no* underground roads and really he had never moved from his burrow!

18

All those other times during the race there had been other stout grandfather-rabbits popping up to taunt the Fox. One brown rabbit, you see, is very much like another and the Fox thought that each one he saw was the Chief-Grandfather Rabbit himself.

"And now," said the Fox to himself, with a yelp, "these terrible rabbits are going to eat me."

But the rabbits had not the slightest intention of eating the Fox. They simply told him to run off and never come back again to the green hills around the clear blue lake. And he never did.

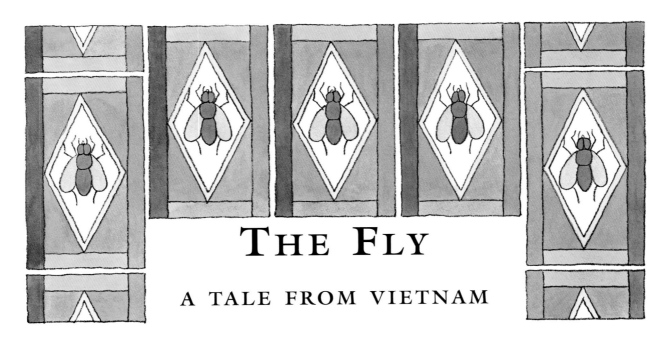

THE FLY

A TALE FROM VIETNAM

EVERYONE IN THE VILLAGE knew the money lender. He was a cunning man and he had become very rich. He lived in a great house, guarded by ferocious dogs. In spite of his enormous wealth, he still went out every day to lend money. The villagers who borrowed his money had to pay back much bigger sums. So almost everyone in the village was in debt to the money lender.

One day the rich man set out for the house of one of the poorest villagers. This lowly laborer worked himself to a shadow, but still could not repay the debt he owed to the money lender.

"If I can't get every penny from that good-for-nothing," grumbled the money lender to

20

himself, "I'll take whatever I can find in his house – furniture, cooking pans or anything else I can lay my hands on."

When the rich man arrived at the house he met a small boy, about eight years old, playing outside. "Child, are your parents at home?" the rich man asked.

"No sir," the boy replied, then went on playing with his sticks and stones, paying no attention whatever to the man.

"Then, where are they?" the rich man asked. He was now getting rather angry with the boy who just went on playing in the dirt.

The rich man had to ask again and only then did the boy look up and slowly reply, "Well sir, my father is cutting living trees to plant dead ones and my mother is at the market selling the wind to buy the moon."

"What on earth are you babbling about?" exploded the rich man. "I'll give you a beating if you don't tell me where they are," he growled, shaking his bamboo walking stick at the boy.

Again, the boy quietly repeated the same answer. The rich man decided to try a different approach. "Now listen to me," he said more gently. "I came here today to get the money your parents owe me. But if you tell me where they really are and what they're doing, I shall not ask for a penny. Is that clear to you?"

This time the boy replied very seriously. "Sir, when you make such an offer you must be joking with me. You're just trying to trick me."

"No, not at all, my child. I promise, as heaven and earth are my witnesses."

But the boy only laughed. "Sir, heaven and earth cannot talk! I want some living thing to be our witness."

Just then the money lender glanced at a jug by the door. There, on the handle, was a fly. Because he was still confident that he was fooling the boy, the rich man announced grandly, "Here is a fly. He can be our witness. Now tell me what you mean about your father cutting living trees to plant dead ones and your mother selling the wind to buy the moon."

The boy looked at the fly sitting on the jug handle. "A fly is a good enough witness for me," he said. "So I shall indeed explain my riddles to you. My father has simply gone to cut down bamboos and make a fence with them for a local farmer. And my mother has gone to the market to sell fans so she can buy oil for our lamps. Isn't that what you'd call selling the wind to buy the moon?"

The rich man nodded. He had to admit this boy was a clever one. "But at least I managed to trick him into using the fly as our witness," thought the money lender as he hurried off.

A few days later he returned in the evening and found the boy's parents at home after a long day's work. He grabbed the boy's father and shook him. "Now you must pay me all the money you owe me," he snarled. "If you don't pay me now I'll take everything you have and your

house as well." The boy pushed between them and cried out, "Father, Father, you don't have to pay your debt. The gentleman promised me that he would forget all about the money you owe him."

"Nonsense," hissed the money lender, "I've never even met this child of yours. Now, are you going to pay me or not?"

The whole dispute was brought before the mandarin who governed that part of the land. The mandarin asked the boy exactly what had happened when the money lender had called. The boy quickly described how he had agreed to explain some riddles to the money lender in order to free his parents from their debt.

But the money lender continued to deny everything. "I've never seen this child before!" he protested.

"How do we know you've not made all this up?" the mandarin now asked the boy. "It's your word against his... If only you had a witness to what happened."

"But I have," said the boy calmly. "A fly."

"Come now, young man. Before me, you must be serious," warned the mandarin sternly.

"But it's true, Your Honor. A fly landed on the money lender's nose just before he made his promise to me..."

Before he could say any more, the money lender had leapt to his feet and, bursting with rage, he snorted, "The fly was not on my nose, he was on the jug handle!" Then he stopped dead and covered his mouth with his hand. But it was too late. Everyone, including the mandarin, started laughing.

"So jug handle or no jug handle, your conversation did happen after all," said the mandarin, pointing at the rich man. "This court says you must keep your promise... Case dismissed!"

Then the mandarin bent down for a word with the boy's parents. "At last this trickster has been tricked. Your son is a very clever boy!"

The poor man and his wife agreed. They gave their son a big hug. Then, knowing that they were now free of their crippling debt, they stepped happily out into the sunshine and walked home to their cottage. And, as for the money lender, he left his great house in disgrace and was never seen in the village again.

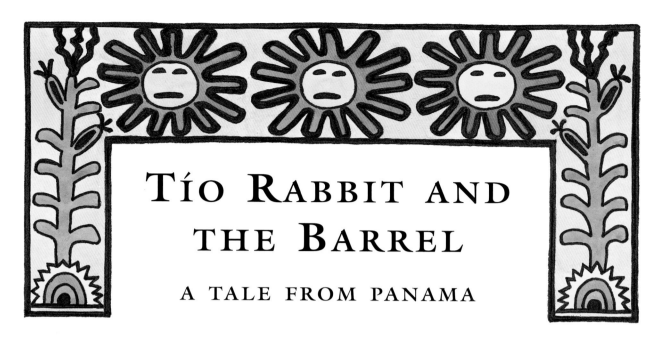

Tío Rabbit and the Barrel

A Tale from Panama

ONE DAY Tío Rabbit was bouncing along the road. He was going off to stay with his grandmother. Suddenly, he came face to face with Tío Jaguar, crouching right in front of him.

"I'm going to eat you!" roared the jaguar.

"Oh come now, Tío Jaguar, there's not much of a meal in me. Just wait until I've been to my grandmother's for a month. I'll have eaten so much of her fine food and I'll be so plump that you won't even recognize me. Let me go on, Tío Jaguar, and you'll see."

Reluctantly, Tío Jaguar let him pass. Tío Rabbit skipped off down the road until suddenly, he ran into Tío Lion.

"I'm going to eat you!" growled the lion, flashing all his big white teeth.

"Well, maybe, Tío Lion, but you'd be making a big mistake. When I come back from my grandmother's I'll have eaten so much that you'll get two juicy meals out of me instead of just one meager one."

"Very well then," said Tío Lion. "But be sure to come back along this road."

So, with a hop and a jump, Tío Rabbit scampered off, until he was stopped by Tío Fox.

"I'm going to eat you!" snarled the fox, licking his lips.

"I advise you to wait, Tío Fox," replied Tío Rabbit.

"When I come back from my grandmother's I'll be so fat that you won't even be able to stretch your jaws around me."

"Very well then," said Tío Fox. "But be sure to return past my den."

At his grandmother's Tío Rabbit filled himself with lettuce, carrots, cabbage and watermelon and, in no time, he was three times as big as when he had arrived. After a month he was ready to go home. His grandmother waved goodbye and called out to him, "Even your own mother won't know you now!"

Just after he'd turned the corner Tío Rabbit grabbed a barrel and jumped inside. Off down the hill it rolled.

And it hadn't rolled far when it bumped past Tío Jaguar. He ran alongside calling out, "Tell me little barrel, have you seen anything of Tío Rabbit?"

From inside the barrel Tío Rabbit disguised his voice and squealed:

"The forest's on fire
Tío Rabbit's burned through.
Run fast, Tío Jaguar,
Or you will burn too!"

Tío Jaguar, believing that the forest really was ablaze, rushed off down the road. Tío Rabbit, in his barrel, rolled after him.

In a while, Tío Lion sprang out from some bushes and roared, "Little barrel, have you come across Tío Rabbit?"

Again Tío Rabbit squeaked in a high-pitched voice:

"The forest's on fire
Tío Rabbit's burned through.
Run fast, Tío Lion,
Or you will burn too!"

Tío Lion panicked at the thought of the advancing flames and raced away as quickly as he could. Tío Rabbit, in his barrel, rolled after him.

A little further on, Tío Fox pounced in front of the barrel and asked, "Little barrel, have you come across Tío Rabbit?"

Again Tío Rabbit squealed:

"The forest's on fire
Tío Rabbit's burned through.
Run fast, Tío Fox
Or you will burn too!"

But the sly Tío Fox wasn't fooled. "I know that voice!" he snarled. "And now I'm going to get you out of that barrel." He bounded along after the rolling barrel, and almost out of breath, he panted, "I'm going to eat you up... ears, tail, voice and all!"

But the barrel gathered more and more speed as it rolled down the hill. Try as he might, Tío Fox just could not keep up with it and finally he collapsed by the side of the road, completely exhausted.

From far away the lazy voice of Tío Rabbit floated back to him, "Adiosito... bye bye, Tío Fox. Watch for me next year when I come home from my grandmother's. Who knows, I might just be bigger than you!"

And, in the distance, Tío Fox could hear the muffled sound of rabbit laughter!

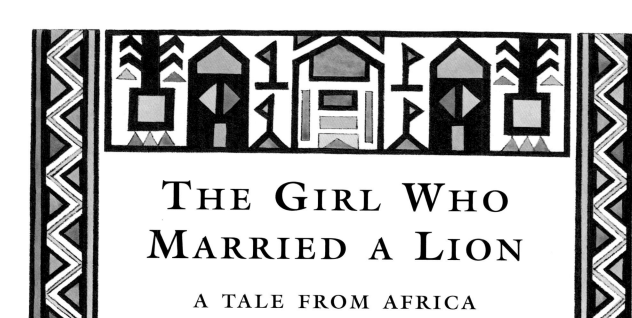

THE GIRL WHO
MARRIED A LION

A TALE FROM AFRICA

KUMALO AND HIS WIFE were very happy when their daughter married. Their new son-in-law had given them many fine cattle as a wedding present. But their own son was not happy. "I think that my sister has married a lion disguised as a man," he whispered angrily to his mother and father. "I refuse to speak to a lion."

Some years passed and the couple had two strong sons, both as handsome as their father. Kumalo and his wife were very proud of their new grandchildren but still their own son muttered and grumbled that he would have nothing to do with his brother-in-law. He felt sure

that one day trouble would come.

Sure enough, the day came when his sister crept back to the family home and confided in her brother, "I'm worried about that husband of mine – I have noticed recently that he smells strange."

So the young man agreed to go with his sister to her hut while her husband was out, and smell some of his things. Sniffing the husband's bag, the brother frowned and said, "That is a lion's scent."

The two hurried back to their father's home. Kumalo didn't like what they told him at all. "That fine young man of yours gave me all those cattle when you married," he said angrily to his daughter. "Where would a lion get such cattle? But if you are sure about your husband really being a lion, we can soon test him," and he bent forward to tell them his plan.

"We'll put a goat outside his hut at night," he said. "If the goat is gone in the morning, then we will know that a lion has eaten it. That will prove that your husband is a lion."

34

So that night they tied a goat outside the hut. The next morning, when Kumalo and his son went to look, there was nothing left but a pile of bones.

"You see," said the son, triumphantly. "No man would eat a goat like that. He is surely a lion!" There was only one thing to do: they fetched their sharpest spears and returned to chase away the son-in-law. Kumalo and his son chased the husband right into the bush and, although they were unable to catch him, the paw prints he left in the dusty soil as he ran for cover were proof enough that he was indeed a lion.

35

Naturally, the daughter was very upset to have lost her fine husband but she had to accept that she had been in danger while she lived with him. After all, what if he had threatened to eat her?

Her brother was still very worried for his sister. What if her two little boys, the nephews he loved so much, turned out to be lions when they grew up? He watched them closely and, although he could see no signs that they might be lions, one day he said to his sister, "We must be quite sure about this. We will have to test your sons, too."

He made a cage out of thin branches and placed it beside a pool where lions always came to drink. Then he led the two boys to the cage and told them to get inside. "I'm testing this cage," he explained to them. "I want to see if it is strong enough to give protection against lions. I'll come back tonight and see if the lions have managed to break into it."

With that, he left his nephews in the cage and hid in some nearby trees to see what would happen.

After a while, two lions walked up to the cage and began to sniff at it. The two boys cowered in a corner of the cage. Then the lions began to roar and they dashed at the cage, shaking its flimsy wooden bars. By now, the two boys were extremely frightened. Seeing all this, the uncle decided that if he didn't leap to their rescue they would surely be eaten.

He rushed towards the lions, waving a long spear to frighten them into the bush.

"Thank you, uncle," the older boy said. "I feared that we would be eaten by those two lions."

37

The uncle smiled as he let his nephews out of the cage. Now he was satisfied that the boys were not lions. For surely, if they had been lions, their attackers would have picked up a familiar scent and would not have tried to break into the cage. Straight away, he told his sister the good news and she hugged her sons warmly.

Years passed and the boys grew up to be strong, kind men. They protected and looked after their beloved mother into her old age and she was always proud to have such fine sons.

WHY THE OWL HAS SUCH BIG EYES

AN ABORIGINAL TALE

WEEMULLEE THE OWL and Willanjee the Hurricane lived out in the desert. They were best friends – always hunting together and cooking, talking and sleeping by the same campfire.

But one thing always bothered Weemullee: he could never see his friend, Willanjee! "You could always change yourself so that I could see you!" Weemullee would often say.

But each time, Willanjee would reply, "No, certainly not. You must never ask to see me. Can you not accept me as your invisible friend?" Then he would sulk silently for a while.

One day, the sun was up early and woke both the Owl and

the Hurricane. "Shall we go hunting?" asked Weemullee.

"Yes," yawned Willanjee. "I'm so hungry – let's start at once."

So off they set. Weemullee carried a spear under his wing and Willanjee had his on his shoulder. Of course, the Hurricane was invisible, but Weemullee knew he was there because he could see the spear floating along beside him. "Look up in that gum tree," said Weemullee, pointing upwards. "A fat opossum. I'll circle around him and chase him down to you."

Willanjee hid behind some rocks, ready with his spear. As soon as the opossum came rushing down the tree trunk, Willanjee rose up from behind the rocks and flung his spear with deadly precision. The opossum fell to the ground with a thud and Weemullee and Willanjee gave cries of triumph. Later in the day they caught some large lizards and another opossum. Together they carried home their catch and cooked a hearty supper. As their campfire began to die down, Weemullee yawned and said, "Time to turn in." They both wrapped their blankets around

themselves and lay down on either side of the fire. But Weemullee could not sleep. He was wondering, as he did every night, that perhaps Willanjee might become visible as he slept under his blanket.

Unable to contain his curiosity any longer, the Owl moved ever so quietly over to the Hurricane. Then, with his eyes open very wide, he turned back the edge of Willanjee's blanket to look... But a terrible thing happened. In the darkness Willanjee thought he was being attacked, so he flung off his blanket and shot into the air. As he swooshed upwards, he tore up bushes, scattered the glowing ashes from the fire and sent clouds of dusty red earth, sticks and stones whirling up into the sky.

Weemullee was swept up into a tree and dragged through its branches, his feathers flying in all directions. He just managed to grab hold of the topmost branch, clinging as tightly as he could until the Hurricane disappeared over the horizon. As he swept on, Willanjee now realised that he must have been startled in the night by Weemullee. It angered him so much that Weemullee had not respected his right to remain invisible that he never came back to live with the Owl again.

Weemullee flew far and wide, calling out for his friend, but he never again heard Willanjee's familiar voice – only the roaring and howling of the Hurricane. And, although the feathers he had lost eventually grew back, his eyes have always remained as big and as round as the moment when he had peered underneath Willanjee's blanket on that terrible night.

THE OLD WOMAN'S ANIMALS

A TALE FROM ASSAM

THERE WAS A TIME when all animals were wild. Although people sometimes saw wild beasts deep in the forests or high up on the mountains, they had not yet started keeping animals to give them milk or carry their heavy loads. All this changed because of an old woman and this is how it happened.

One evening, she was on her way back from the rice fields to cook supper for her daughter. Suddenly, the old woman felt a pair of hands cover her eyes. It was a spirit called Zize. "I'll let you go if you'll give me your daughter to be my wife," he said. The old woman agreed and early the next day, the spirit carried off the girl. A year went by and then the girl came back to see her mother. After a few days she said to the old woman, "Please come back with me now, and spend some time in my new home."

So mother and daughter set off to the spirit's house. The old woman took care to mark the way by dropping a trail of rice husks.

The girl and her mother spent many happy weeks together in the spirit's house. A day or two before it was time for the old woman to go home, her daughter whispered, "When you leave, as a going-away present, ask the spirit for the little basket that hangs beside the front door."

So, later, when the time came for her to go, the old woman asked Zize for the little basket. At first he refused, quite firmly, but then he turned to her and spoke gravely, "Very well. You may have it but you must not open it on your way home and when you do get home, you must build a fence around the basket before you take off the lid."

The old woman thanked her daughter and Zize for their warm hospitality and also for the little basket. But, as she followed the trail of rice husks back through the forest, she wondered what could possibly be inside the basket. After a while, she could contain her curiosity no longer and she put down the basket to lift open its lid. As she bent over it, she heard growling, tweeting and squeaking and, before she could close the basket, out leapt bears, birds, mice and monkeys. And what a commotion as they all rushed out from the open basket into the forest! Finally, the old woman managed to throw herself onto the basket and close the lid. She held it down firmly and re-tied the string to keep it shut. She could just hear some more animal sounds from inside the little basket. "There must still be a few animals inside," she said to herself. "I heard some mooing and grunting and barking."

The old woman paused for a while to get her breath back and then she picked up the basket and continued her journey home, following the trail of rice husks. It was daybreak when she finally trudged into her village. The old woman woke her neighbors and they all helped her to build a fence around the basket, just as the spirit Zize had told her.

46

Then, carefully, she opened the basket and out came... cows, horses, sheep, buffaloes, pigs, chickens and dogs. They all wanted to rush off, just as the other animals had done, but, of course, now there was a fence to stop them. The old woman and her neighbors collected up food for these animals to eat and brought water from the stream for them to drink. After a week or so the animals had all settled down happily. This was now their new home and they liked it here.

A year later the old woman's daughter paid her another visit, this time with her husband. As they walked into the village they passed neatly-fenced fields and little bamboo shelters for the animals and their young.

And so, that is why some animals are wild and some live with people. Perhaps, if the old woman had not been so hasty in opening her basket on her way home, then all the animals that are still wild would be tamed and living with us, too!

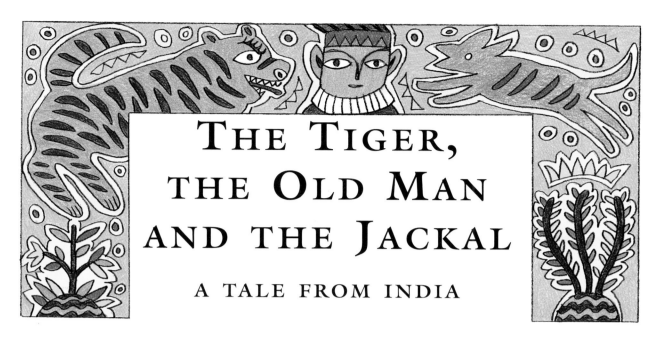

THE TIGER,
THE OLD MAN
AND THE JACKAL

A TALE FROM INDIA

ONCE UPON A TIME there was a tiger who had been caught in a trap. The trap was a cage and, when the door slammed shut, the tiger tried in vain to gnaw through the bars but he couldn't get out. Just then an old man walked by.

"Old man, please let me out of this cage," cried the tiger.

"Well, no," replied the old man gently. "If I did, you'd probably eat me."

"Not at all," pleaded the tiger. "I'd be so grateful I would be your slave forever!" With this, the tiger started to sob and sigh and weep so that the soft-hearted old man decided to open the door of the cage. Out popped the tiger and, seizing the poor old man, he cried, "What a fool you are! I've been in there so long and I'm now so hungry that I'm going to have to eat you up!"

The old man begged the tiger not to eat him. "Let me ask the first three things I come across what they think. They'll decide for us whether you might eat me or not." The tiger agreed and the old man moved nervously towards the shade of a huge old tree. The old man asked this old shady tree what it thought of the matter.

"What have you to complain about?" grumbled the tree.

"I give shade and shelter to everyone who passes by and what do they do in return? They tear down my branches to feed to their cattle! So don't whimper – be a man!"

Then the old man walked on to where a buffalo was yoked to a heavy stone wheel for grinding corn. He asked the buffalo what he thought and it answered, "You're a fool to expect mercy. Look at me! While I gave them milk, my owners fed me on cotton-seed and oil-cake; but now that I'm old, they set me to work all day grinding their corn and feed me on nothing more than scraps of garbage."

So the old man knelt down and asked the road beneath his feet what it thought of the matter.

"My dear sir, you are a fool to expect anything else! Here I am, useful to everybody, yet all of them, rich and poor, never thank me. They just trample on me and give me nothing but ashes from their pipes and husks of grain from their carts."

The old man looked glum and was about to return to the tiger when there in front of him stood a jackal. "Whoa there, old man. What's the matter?" it asked. "You look as miserable as a fish out of water."

51

The old man told him everything but still the jackal shook his head and said that he was a little confused.

"Maybe we should go back to where this all started. Then I can tell you what I think should happen."

So they both returned to the cage where they found the tiger, sitting beside it, sharpening his claws and licking his lips. "Dinner time, and I think that means you – old man!" he growled.

"Just give me five minutes," pleaded the old man. "I have to explain everything to our friend here – the jackal." And then, whispering to the tiger, "He's a bit slow in understanding things."

The tiger agreed to this and the old man began the story all over again, not missing a single thing and making it all last as long as possible.

"Oh, oh," cried the jackal, "I'm still so confused. You were in the cage and the tiger came walking by..."

"Rrrah," growled the tiger, "what a fool you are! I was in the cage."

"Of course!" cried the jackal, pretending to tremble with fright. "Yes! I was in the cage – no I wasn't – oh dear! Where are my wits? Let me see – the tiger was in the old man and the cage came walking by – no, that's not it either. Oh, I shall never understand!"

"I'll make you understand!" roared the tiger. "Look here – I am the tiger."

"Yes," answered the jackal.

"And that is the old man."

"I see."

"And that's the cage."

"Right."

"And I was in the cage – do you understand?"

"Well yes – no – I mean – how did you get in there?"

"How!" growled the tiger.

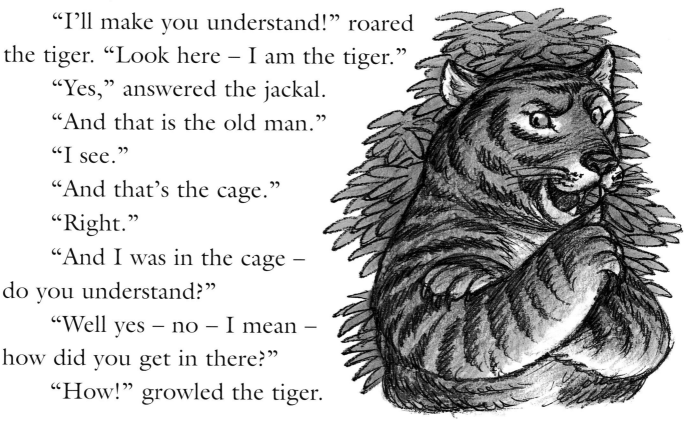

53

"Why in the usual way, of course!"

"Oh, I'm getting all confused again. What is the usual way?"

At this the tiger lost his patience, and, jumping into the cage, cried, "This way! Now do you understand how it was?"

"Perfectly!" laughed the jackal as he snapped the door of the cage shut. "Now, if you'll permit me to say so, I think we'll leave things just the way they were!"

THREE BALLS OF WOOL

A PERSIAN TALE

LONG AGO THERE lived in Persia a poor housewife called Mara. Each day she would go out looking for herbs and spices to flavor the meals she made for her husband and baby daughter. One day she happened to wander into a palace garden. It looked very overgrown and everywhere rotten fruit lay on the ground. "What a waste," said Mara to herself as she bent down to gather up some figs.

But the moment she touched the fruit, the ground started to shake and smoke rose up from the soil.

Suddenly, there appeared a horrible witch with three warts on her nose and five scars on her chin.

"You're stealing my fruit!" screamed the witch. "Now you must pay me one hundred gold coins."

"But I have nothing in this world except an old cooking pot and a hungry husband and baby."

"I've no use for cooking pots or men," cackled the witch. "So you'll have to give me your baby."

"Oh, I cannot!" cried Mara. The witch was now furious and green smoke curled from her mouth.

"You must give me your baby or I shall destroy this whole village!" And with that, she lifted her arms as if they were wings and vanished in a huge ball of fire.

Mara collapsed with fear. When she came round she was back home, lying on her mattress, thinking that it all must have been a dream.

Time passed and life became better for Mara. Her husband traveled far and wide as a merchant and earned enough money for them to buy a fine villa in a neighboring village, overlooking the sea. Their baby daughter, Leila, grew up to be the most beautiful girl in all of Persia.

56

One day, Leila was playing hide-and-seek with her friends in the fields when she noticed a purple butterfly. It had a strange pattern on its wings – three dots on one wing and five lines on the other. Leila reached out to touch it and, when she did, the ground shook and the butterfly turned into a witch with three warts on her nose and five scars on her chin.

"Got you at last!" screamed the witch, grabbing Leila and throwing her into a black coach. Poor Leila was taken to the witch's palace and locked up in a tiny room where she had to spend all day knitting. The witch gave her very little to eat – just a daily portion of cold couscous and a few dried figs.

"I have not kidnapped you," said the witch. "Your mother promised you to me as payment for some figs I sold her many years ago."

Leila said nothing. She didn't know what to think. She was certainly very afraid of this ugly witch with her warts and scars. Seven whole years went by and, as the time passed, Leila learned some of the old witch's magic by watching her closely. She found that she was able to cast some simple spells like changing people into bottles or making flowers dance around the room.

Every day the witch would go out to buy food. Since there were no doors in the palace, she would fly out of one of the windows. When she wanted to come back in again, she would call out to Leila and sing:

"Leila, Leila,
Sweet and fair:
Granny's coming,
Let down your hair!"

Then Leila would let down her long hair through the window and the witch would climb up.

58

The witch started trusting Leila more and more but there were still three things the girl was forbidden to do. She was not allowed to open the chest under the palace stairs, to look at herself in the mirror on the palace wall or gaze out of the window.

One day, while the witch was out, Leila opened the forbidden chest. Inside she found three balls of wool – blue, green and red. "Is that all?" thought Leila to herself as she closed the chest and went on with her knitting.

The next day she looked into the forbidden mirror. "Three balls of wool are the source of the witch's magic!" came a voice from the mirror. "They have the power to help you escape from danger."

When the witch came home that evening, she seemed to look suspiciously at Leila. It was almost as if she suspected something.

The next day, Leila gazed out of the forbidden window. The street below was full of people. Leila saw a young man in the crowd who stopped and waved to her. Then he came over to the palace wall and called:

"Leila, Leila,

Sweet and fair:

Someone's coming,

Let down your hair!"

Leila let down her hair and the young man climbed up. "I've often heard the witch singing that song," he explained. "Now, at last, I've managed to reach you."

Leila told him the whole of her sad story. The young man, who was a prince from another country, was very angry. "I'll send for my father's army and the soldiers will tear down this palace and save you," he said.

Just then, the witch came back and called out from below. Leila quickly kissed the prince and, with some of the magic she'd learned, turned him into a shawl.

The witch came through the window and into the room and started to sniff. "I smell people!" she screeched. "Leila, have you looked out of the window?"

Leila shook her head. "No, Grandma, I've been busy knitting all day and, look, I've made you this lovely shawl!" The witch grabbed the shawl and hung it on a hook.

When the witch went out the next day, Leila turned the shawl back into the prince. Acting quickly, he fetched all the sheets in the palace and twisted them into a rope. Leila took the three balls of wool from the chest and put them in her pocket. Then the two of them climbed down the rope and escaped.

On her return in the evening, the witch called out but, this time, no hair came tumbling down. The witch guessed that Leila must have escaped. She filled one of her shoes with water and looked into it. "Aha," she cried, "my Leila is running across the desert." Then she snatched her magic stick and set off faster than

the wind to catch Leila and the prince. But Leila saw her coming: she took the green ball of wool and flung it behind her. Suddenly, a dense green forest of thorny trees appeared and the witch was caught up in it. The two hurried on but, around midnight, they looked back to see that the witch had chewed her way out of the thorny forest with her sharp teeth and was again swooping towards them.

"Throw the blue ball!" cried the prince.

Leila threw it and, suddenly, there was a vast blue ocean with waves that swept the witch head-over-heels and she began to sink. At dawn the two looked back, this time astonished to see that the witch had drunk the whole ocean. She was still following them.

Desperately, Leila threw the red ball. A wall of red fire appeared and the witch was trapped inside it. "I'll put out the flames," screamed the witch. But this time, before she could mutter a magic spell, she was burned to a cinder.

Leila and the prince stopped to rest under a palm tree. Then they happily continued their journey to the prince's kingdom. The people there greeted them with flowers and fruit and singing and dancing. Leila sent for her parents and, together, all four of them lived in peace for many happy years.

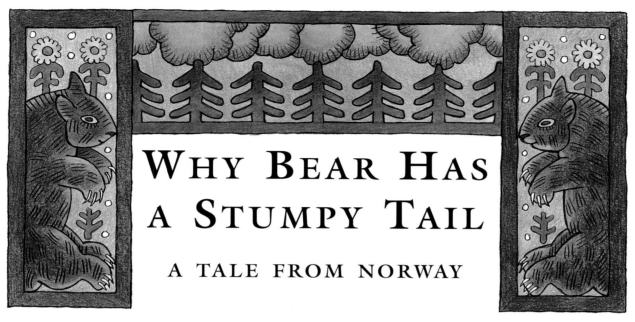

WHY BEAR HAS A STUMPY TAIL

A TALE FROM NORWAY

ONG, LONG AGO, at the beginning of the world, Bear had a truly magnificent tail. He had been at the end of the line when the ears were being handed out, so he was given only the smallest, stubbiest ears. After he'd been given his ears he was so tired from all the waiting that he fell asleep. But, when he woke up, he was surprised to discover that he was at the front of the line for tails.

Of course, Bear chose the best tail there was – long and thick and wavy. "What a wonderful tail!" he said to himself. "I shall be able to fan myself in the heat, keep the flies away and, perhaps, even learn to hold things with it."

Now Fox had pushed his way to the front of the line and chosen a fine pair of tufty ears and a fiery, bushy tail for himself. But he was still very envious and begrudged Bear his spectacular tail.

One day, in the freezing cold of a very long, hard winter, Bear was searching for grubs under a rotten log. He was just about to give up the search and sleep for the rest of the winter when, suddenly, Fox appeared. His mouth was stuffed with fish.

"Where on earth did you get those?" Bear asked. He loved fish but he found it so difficult to catch them.

Fox stopped, then backed away nervously – he hadn't seen Bear behind the log and now he realized that he might lose all his fish.

"I wish I could catch fish like that," said Bear, looking longingly at them. "I don't suppose…"

"But, of course!" said Fox quickly. "I'll tell you how to do it. With a tail like yours, you'll catch more fish than you can eat!"

"What's my tail got to do with it?" questioned Bear.

"Well, I caught all these in a couple of hours and my tail's not nearly as big and bushy as yours. Of course it got a bit cold but, there you are. The longer you can stick it out, the better your catch will be."

Bear squinted suspiciously at Fox. "You have not even begun to explain how it's done," he said and their noses nearly touched.

"I haven't?" replied Fox. "Oh, I'm sorry. What exactly didn't you understand?"

"All of it," growled Bear. "Especially the bits you missed out."

"Oh, I see. Well," began Fox, "first you go down to the river, or the lake, or the sea, or anywhere where there's water with fish in it and, then, you cut a hole in it."

"In the water?" spluttered Bear.

"No, in the ice! It's winter, remember? You cut a hole in the ice and lower your tail through and wave it about a little to attract attention. Then you just wait... for as long as you can. It might sting a bit but that's just the fish biting. Remember, the longer you wait, the more fish you'll get."

"It sounds easy," said Bear. "What's the catch?"

"Enough fish to last you for weeks!" laughed Fox. "But there is just one thing."

"Oh, and what's that?" asked Bear.

"Well if you take your tail out slowly, for some

reason, the fish just drop off. So, if you want to keep all the fish you've caught, jerk it out suddenly as if you're leaping over the moon!"

"Very well," said Bear, firmly. "Be certain to come by tomorrow and see what I've caught," and he hurried off to a frozen stream nearby.

There, he did exactly as Fox had told him. He lowered his tail through a hole in the ice and waited for the rest of the day and most of the night, too.

Bear sat on the ice for so long that his tail was completely frozen in. Then he eyed the moon above the trees and gave the biggest, strongest leap he'd ever made. And... his tail snapped off! Bear rushed home, howling all the way, to wait for Fox. Of course, Bear may have had no fish to show but he did want to show Fox just how angry he was. Bear waited in vain, for Fox never came along.

All this happened long, long ago but, to this day, bears have short, stumpy tails and foxes always stay well out of their way!

THE CAT, THE ROOSTER AND THE SCYTHE

A CZECH TALE

ONCE UPON A TIME there were three brothers. The eldest was called Marty, the second was called Matt and the youngest was called Michael. Their father, who had never been a rich man, died leaving them a little cottage to live in and a cat, a rooster and a scythe. Marty took the scythe because he was strong enough to use it, Matt took the rooster and Michael took the cat.

One day, Marty told his brothers, "We can't just stay in this cottage, doing nothing. Tomorrow I shall go out into the world with my scythe."

So the next day he went off with his scythe, leaving Matt and

70

Michael to look after the house. He traveled far and wide looking for work but found nothing until, at last, he came to a faraway country where the people were strangely simple and spoke in an accent that Marty could hardly understand.

A group of them gathered around Marty and asked, "What have you there and what is it for?"

"This is a scythe," answered Marty. "I can cut long grass with it."

"How wonderful!" they said. "We have to pull up the long grass with our own hands." They took him straight away to see their king and to show him the scythe. Then Marty was set to work cutting the long grass in the meadows around the castle.

"You must all go away to leave me and my amazing scythe to do our work," he explained. "At lunchtime we will both need a hearty meal."

So, at midday, the simple folk brought two plates piled high with food which they left for Marty and his scythe to eat.

"This is a grand idea," thought Marty as he polished off all the food himself. "I'm certainly going to get plenty to eat working for these simple folk and their king!"

After a few days, Marty had finished cutting all the grass in the meadows around the castle. He went to the king to be paid for his work.

"Does that knife of yours cut the grass by itself?" asked the king.

"Yes, it does, Your Majesty," replied Marty.

"Would you be willing to sell it to us for a thousand gold pieces?" continued the king.

"Well, it's worth more, but I'll let you have it for a thousand," agreed Marty. He laid down the scythe on a cushion before the king, took the bag of money and returned to his brothers and their humble cottage.

After a year, all the grass around the castle had grown very long again. So the king commanded his people to take the scythe out into the meadows and leave it there to do its work. The simple folk remembered that the scythe needed to be fed, so they returned at midday with a plate piled high with all kinds of delicious foods. They were surprised to see that not a single blade of grass had been cut, so one of them said, "Maybe we should all beat it with sticks to make it work harder."

"No," replied another, "let's leave the scythe to eat its lunch and return at sunset to see whether it has worked better after a hearty meal."

But at sunset, still no grass had been cut and even the lunch hadn't been touched. This time the king had come out to see what was going on. "It cut a lot of grass when

Marty was here," he said, bending down to look at the scythe very closely. "Maybe it's bewitched. Let's give it a beating and if it still doesn't cut the grass, we'll bury it."

The simple folk obeyed the king's command and set about beating the scythe with sticks but it bounced up and nearly cut them. "Oh," they cried. "It really is bewitched." Reluctantly, they buried the scythe and went back to pulling up the long grass with their hands as they'd done before.

Meanwhile, the brothers were all happily spending the money that Marty had brought home. Before long it was all gone and Matt said, "Now I must go out into the world with my rooster. Perhaps I can get a good price for him, just as you did with your scythe."

As Matt set off, Marty called out to him, "Go to the country with the simple people and their strange accent."

After many days, Matt arrived in the country and was greeted by the simple folk. One of them stepped forward and asked what kind of bird he had under his arm.

"This is a rooster," replied Matt.

"And what does a rooster do?" asked the simple man.

Matt whispered in the man's ear, "This bird can tell the time. It tells you when it's morning."

"Oh!" gasped the man. "Here we never know what time it is. Our king would pay a fortune for a bird who could tell us all when it's morning."

So Matt and his rooster were taken to the king. The simple courtiers told the king that there was a man with a crowing bird that tells you when it's morning.

The king was delighted and commanded a golden house to be made for the bird. Everyone was anxious to discover if the rooster would indeed tell them when it was morning. Sure enough, as night was falling the rooster

went to sleep, and then at four o'clock, when the day was just dawning, the rooster let out a loud, clear crow.

The king and all his subjects leapt out of bed. The sound of the rooster was something they'd never heard before: they were very impressed. The king gave Matt five thousand gold pieces for his magical bird. Matt thanked the king warmly and went home to his brothers. Once again, they shared out the money and they all enjoyed spending it. And once again, it was not long before the money ran out. Michael said, "Now it's my turn to go to the kingdom with the simple people and their strange language. I shall take them my cat."

Michael traveled for many days until he heard people talking with an unfamiliar accent. He knew that he had arrived in the country his brothers had already visited. "What's that you have in your basket?" asked a man sitting on a wall.

"This is a very clever animal," said Michael, opening the basket. "If you've any mice in your house, he'll catch them all in no time."

"Our king would be very interested in your clever animal.

In the castle there are many, many rooms and they're all full of mice. I'll take you to the king right away."

The king was indeed surprised and delighted by Michael's clever animal, especially when he heard that it would get rid of all the mice in the castle. The king peeped into the basket and whispered to Michael, "We'll put this cat, as you call this animal, to the test. If he gets rid of all the mice in my bedroom then I'll pay you ten thousand pieces of gold for him. We'll keep him here in the castle and he can get rid of all the mice forever."

Sure enough, Michael's cat quickly killed all the mice in the king's bedroom. "And he's eaten them all up!" exclaimed the courtiers. "Now we don't even have to feed him."

Michael set off home to his brothers with the money he'd been given for the cat. The cat, meanwhile, set to work catching all the mice in the castle and eating them up. The king was extremely pleased but then, when the cat had cleared the very last room of mice, he became a little worried. "What will our amazing cat eat now?" he pondered. He snapped his fingers and commanded a messenger to race after Michael and ask him what the cat would eat now that all the mice had gone.

The messenger rode furiously for a night and a day and finally caught up with Michael. "Stop, stop!" he shouted. Then he started to gabble his question, "His Majesty," began the messenger, "wishes to know what the cat will eat... when there are no mice left..."

Michael could hardly understand what the man was saying. "His Majesty..." he said, starting to repeat the messenger's words and trying to decipher them for himself. But he had not managed to say any more before the messenger turned sharply and galloped off in a terrible panic.

Breathless and covered in dust, the messenger arrived back at the castle. He raced into the king's council chamber and cried, "Bad news, Your Majesty."

"What did he say?" demanded the king.

"He said that when the cat has eaten all the mice it will eat... Your Majesty!" replied the messenger, trembling.

"Lock up that cat at the top of the tallest tower!" roared the king. "Let him be guarded night and day by two of my fiercest soldiers."

From the small window in his cell, the cat gazed longingly over fields and barns where there would be many more mice to hunt. When the fearsome guards opened the door to give him some water, he darted between their legs, raced down the spiral staircase and leapt from the castle walls to freedom.

The guards, dropping the jug of water in their fright, rushed to tell the king. "Your Majesty," they whimpered, "that fearsome animal has escaped!"

The king sent his guards to search every corner of his kingdom for the cat – but he was never found.

Perhaps he lived out the rest of his days in a cosy farmhouse kitchen, far from that strange land, lapping up saucers of creamy milk and purring happily.

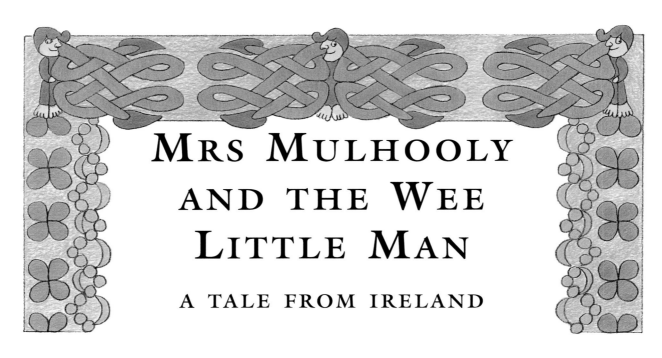

MRS MULHOOLY AND THE WEE LITTLE MAN

A TALE FROM IRELAND

MRS MULHOOLY was sitting up late one night, when she thought she heard someone in the room with her whispering, "Hurry up! Hurry up!"

It was past ten o'clock and she had been sitting by the fire doing some spinning. She looked over to her tabby cat and said, "I don't want to hurry up. I'm happy staying up late by the fire."

The big tabby cat just yawned and licked his whiskers as if to say, "It's nothing to do with me."

And now Mrs Mulhooly was sure that she saw a little somebody or something scampering across the floor.

"That was not a mouse or a rat because it had two legs, not four," she said. "Maybe it was a bird that flew in by mistake." Mrs Mulhooly opened the door a little to let it outside again and she stepped outside for a few moments, enjoying the night air. As she turned to come back inside, she caught sight of her tabby cat through the window. He was curled up by the fire, waving his tail and purring gently, as if he was meeting someone he knew!

As she came back into the room, Mrs Mulhooly found her cat sitting beside a crack in the wall – watching something most intently but all the while purring happily.

"There is something very odd about the house tonight," said Mrs Mulhooly as she climbed the ladder to her little attic bedroom.

The following night the house seemed even stranger. Everything seemed to go wrong. When Mrs Mulhooly sat down to spin, her wool tangled and knotted. Then a spark from the fire jumped out onto her wool and it began to smoke. As Mrs Mulhooly leapt up to stamp it out, she upset the cat's saucer of milk and

suddenly there was ash and milk all over the hearth. "What a mess!" grumbled Mrs Mulhooly as she wiped the fireplace but, as she did so, she felt sure that someone was watching her. "There's just no peace in this house at all, at all," complained Mrs Mulhooly. "I'm going to have an early night." And, even though it was just half-past nine, she climbed up the ladder to her attic.

But Mrs Mulhooly just couldn't sleep. Her big tabby cat padded up the ladder to join her and he took up most of the bed. After a very bad night, Mrs Mulhooly climbed downstairs to find her kitchen in a terrible state. There were ashes all over the floor, pools of water spilt from the bucket by the door and the yarn on her spinning-wheel was all of a tangle while the unspun wool lay in a soggy, dirty heap.

"There's something very odd indeed going on in this house," muttered Mrs Mulhooly as she looked at the mess. "Maybe the Wise Woman down the valley can tell me what's going on?"

So she set off to see the Wise Woman, taking a skein
of her thickest, softest wool to give her as a present.
The Wise Woman was delighted with the wool and asked
Mrs Mulhooly to sit down and explain what was troubling
her. When she finished, the Wise Woman thought for
a while then, nodding her head, said quietly, "As the
evenings are getting cold and frosty, there is someone else
who wants to share your warm hearth. Go up to bed at
nine o'clock tonight but sit at the top of the ladder and
watch for a while. You'll see what you'll see."

Mrs Mulhooly went home and that night, when the
clock was at five minutes to nine, she put away her
spinning-wheel and went up the ladder to bed. Just as the
Wise Woman had said, she knelt down to watch the room

below. She could see her tabby cat purring and pawing at the crack in the wall. Suddenly, from the crack popped a wee little man with a pointed red cap and all dressed in green. He carried a wee leather bag with some tools in. He chuckled to himself as he held out his hands 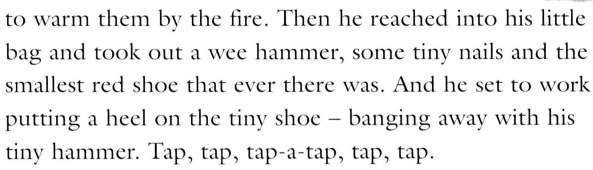 to warm them by the fire. Then he reached into his little bag and took out a wee hammer, some tiny nails and the smallest red shoe that ever there was. And he set to work putting a heel on the tiny shoe – banging away with his tiny hammer. Tap, tap, tap-a-tap, tap, tap.

"So that's who it was!" thought Mrs Mulhooly as she looked down and watched him working away contentedly. "Well, he's welcome to work there by the fire all winter long," she said to herself as she snuggled into her bed.

In the morning, when she came down to make breakfast, her tabby cat purred happily. It was as if he knew that the wee little man was now one of the family.

When the first warm days of spring arrived, Mrs Mulhooly became a grandmother. She knitted a beautiful, soft shawl for her granddaughter and she also gave her the loveliest little pair of red shoes. They fitted the baby perfectly.

And who could have made these tiny shoes? The wee little man, of course!

THE ROSE OF PITY

A TALE FROM ITALY

ONCE UPON A TIME there was a rich merchant who lived in Italy. Every month his ships came home laden with goods from far-off lands, and then they would sail away with cargoes of fine Italian cloth and wines. And so it was that the merchant grew richer and richer.

Now this man had three daughters – Assunta, Carolina and Bellindia. Assunta and Carolina were selfish and proud and thought only of themselves. Bellindia was kind and gentle and always thought first of other people.

One day the merchant had to ride off to a distant port to greet one of his ships that had arrived there.

He asked his daughters what presents they would like him to bring back for them. Assunta and Carolina each wanted precious silk dresses, but Bellindia asked only for a little white rose bush.

When the merchant came to the far-away port, his ship had unloaded and, pleased with the cargo, he hurried to the nearby market and bought two of the finest silk dresses for Assunta and Carolina. But somehow he quite forgot about Bellindia's little rose bush.

Riding home, the merchant was so busy thinking about the next ship to sail home that he went off along the wrong road. Soon he was in a deep, dark forest and completely lost. Eventually, he came to a great mansion, all overgrown and silent. He tied up his horse and pushed open the huge front door. It seemed quite deserted, but in the gloom he could just make out a rough wooden bed. He tiptoed over and lay down to sleep.

Imagine his surprise when he awoke the next morning and there beside his bed was a delicious breakfast ready for him to eat. But still there was no one to be seen.

When he went outside he found that his horse had been well fed and beautifully groomed. As he led his horse to the gate his eye fell on a little white rose bush and in a flash he remembered Bellindia's request.

Glancing to right and left and seeing no one, the merchant bent down to pull out the pretty bush. Just then, there was a tug on his elbow and he looked up to see a truly ugly and fierce-looking wizard who hissed at him angrily, "Have you no shame? You've enjoyed my house and my hospitality, and now you steal my roses!"

The merchant blushed and told the wizard the story of Bellindia's wish.

As he listened, the wizard's harsh looks softened. "Bellindia," he said quietly; "what a gentle name!"

"For a sweet and gentle person," her father answered.

"Go home," said the wizard, "and tell Bellindia she must come here herself if she wishes to own my little rose bush."

So the merchant hurried home and gave Bellindia the wizard's message. Though her sisters laughed and said the whole idea was ridiculous, Bellindia liked the wizard's message and gladly set out with her father to collect the little white rose bush.

This time the merchant remembered the right road into the forest and soon they found the wizard's mysterious mansion. Yet, search as he would, the merchant could no longer find the little white rose bush. They stayed on for many days but still they couldn't find it. Nor was there any sign of the wizard nor of any servants, yet each and every day magnificent meals would appear as if by magic. And on the tray for Bellindia there would always be dozens of white roses with a card written in gold – *For Bellindia.*

By now the merchant had become impatient to return home and check his fleet of ships. "We'll never find that rose bush, Bellindia. Be ready to ride off, first thing in the morning," he said angrily.

Now Bellindia had grown to love the great silent mansion, and, sitting by a shady pool in the garden, she cried a little. Just as her tears began to splash down into the water, a shadow appeared in front of her and she looked up, startled.

It was the wizard and, alas, he was ten times uglier than she had ever dreamed. But Bellindia was too kind to hurt his feelings, so she looked at him calmly as though she were not afraid.

The wizard asked her, "Have you enjoyed my house and the roses I've sent you each day? Are you happy here?"

"Oh yes, very happy. Indeed I've spent many a pleasant hour in the garden looking for the bush that those white roses come from," Bellindia replied gently.

"Indeed," said the wizard. "Then will you marry me?"

But Bellindia, seeing how ugly and fearsome he looked, answered, "No, I cannot."

At this, the wizard fell to the ground in great distress, clutching at his heart. Bellindia bent over him and, at the sight of his pale face and his sunken eyes, she feared he might be about to die. She remembered all his kindness to her and whispered, "If only you might live, I would marry you now!"

Then suddenly beside Bellindia there grew up a little white rose bush, and at the same moment the wizard's eyes opened.

"And now can we be married?" he asked quietly and smiled.

"Yes, I will marry you now," Bellindia replied, giving him a white rose from the little bush.

"It is called the Rose of Pity," said the wizard, "but now I will rename it the Rose of Love."

95

And before Bellindia's eyes, the rose changed from pure white to deepest crimson. And – even more astonishing – as it did so, the wizard changed into a handsome man, as tall and strong as a king. He told the surprised Bellindia the whole story of how he had been under a spell, doomed to remain ugly until some fair maiden's pity could break the enchantment.

So Bellindia and the wizard were married and now live happily in the great house with a courtyard filled with red and white rosebushes.